Editors: Ann Redpath, Etienne Delessert
Art Director: Rita Marshall
Publisher: George R. Peterson, Jr.

Copyright © 1984 Creative Education, Inc., 123 S. Broad Street,
Mankato, Minnesota 56001, USA. American Edition.
Copyright © 1984 Grasset & Fasquelle, Paris – Editions 24 Heures, Lausanne. French Edition.
International copyrights reserved in all countries.

Library of Congress Catalog Card No.: 83-71185
Grimm, Jakob and Wilhelm; Snow White and Rose Red
Mankato, MN: Creative Education, Inc.; 32 pages. ISBN: 0-87191-938-9

Color separations by Photolitho A.G., Gossau/Zurich
Printed in Switzerland by Imprimeries Réunies S.A. Lausanne.

SNOW WHITE AND ROSE RED

JAKOB & WILHELM GRIMM
illustrated by
ROLAND TOPOR

CREATIVE EDUCATION INC.

ECIA 1981 Chapter II
Proj. No. 094-C2-85

A POOR widow lived in a little cottage with a garden in front of it, in which grew two rose trees, one bearing white roses and the other red. She had two children, who were just like the two rose trees; one was called Snow White and the other Rose Red, and they were the sweetest and best children in the world, always diligent and always cheerful; but Snow White was quieter and more gentle than Rose Red. Rose Red loved to run about the fields and meadows, and to pick flowers and catch butterflies; but Snow White sat at home with her mother and helped her in the household, or read aloud to her when there was no work to do.

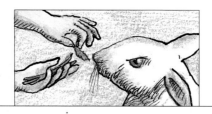

The two children loved each other so dearly that they always walked about hand in hand whenever they went out together, and when Snow White said: "We will never desert each other," Rose Red answered: "No, not as long as we live." And the mother added: "Whatever one gets she shall share with the other."

They often roamed about in the woods gathering berries and no beast offered to hurt them; on the contrary, the animals came up to them in the most confiding manner. The little hare would eat a cabbage leaf from their hands, the deer grazed beside them, the stag would bound past them merrily, and the birds remained on the branches and sang to them with all their might. No evil ever befell them. If they tarried late in the wood and night overtook them, they lay down together on the moss and slept till morning, and their mother knew they were quite safe, and never felt anxious about them.

Once, when they had slept the night in the wood and had been wakened by the morning sun, they perceived a beautiful child in a shining white robe sitting close to their resting place. The figure got up, looked at them kindly, but said nothing, and vanished into the wood. And when they looked round about them they became aware that they had slept quite close to a precipice, over which they would certainly have fallen had they gone on a few steps further in the darkness. And when they told their mother of their adventure, she said what they had seen must have been the angel that guards good children.

Snow White and Rose Red kept their mother's cottage so beautifully clean and neat that it was a pleasure to go into it. In summer Rose Red looked after the house, and every morning before her mother awoke she placed a bunch of flowers before the bed, with a rose from each tree. In winter Snow White lit the fire and put on the kettle, which was made of brass, but so beautifully polished that it shone like gold. In the evening when the snowflakes fell their mother said:

"Snow White, go and close the shutters." And they drew round the fire, while the mother put on her spectacles and read aloud from a big book and the two girls listened and sat and spun. Beside them on the ground lay a little lamb, and behind them perched a little, white dove with its head tucked under its wings.

One evening as they sat thus cozily together, someone knocked at the door as though he desired admittance. The mother said:

"Rose Red, open the door quickly; it must be some traveller seeking shelter."

Rose Red hastened to unbar the door, and thought she saw a poor man standing in the darkness outside; but it was no such thing, only a bear, who poked his thick, black head through the door. Rose Red screamed aloud and sprang back in terror, the lamb began to bleat, the dove flapped its wings, and Snow White ran and hid behind her mother's bed. But the bear began to speak, and said:

"Don't be afraid, I won't hurt you. I am half frozen, and only wish to warm myself a little."

"My poor bear," said the mother, "lie down by the fire, only take care you don't burn your fur." Then she called out: "Snow White and Rose Red, come out; the bear will do you no harm: he is a good, honest creature."

So they both came out of their hiding-places, and gradually the lamb and dove drew near too, and they all forgot their fear. The bear asked the children to beat the snow a little out of his fur, and they fetched a brush and scrubbed him till he was dry. Then the beast stretched himself in front of the fire, and growled quite happily and comfortably. The children soon grew quite at their ease with him and played with their helpless guest. They tugged his fur with their hands, put their small feet on his back, and rolled him about here and there, or took a hazel wand and beat him with it; and if he growled they only laughed. The bear submitted to everything with the best possible good nature, only when they went too far he cried:

"Snow White and Rose Red,
Don't beat your lover dead."

When it was time to retire for the night, and the others went to bed, the mother said to the bear:

"You can lie there on the hearth, in heaven's name; it will be shelter for you from the cold and wet."

As soon as day dawned the children let him out, and he trotted over the snow into the wood.

From this time on the bear came every evening at the same hour, and lay down by the hearth and let the children play what pranks they liked with him; and they got so accustomed to him that the door was never shut till their friend had made his appearance.

When spring came, and all outside was green, the bear said one morning to Snow White:

"Now I must go away, and not return again the whole summer."

"Where are you going to, dear bear?" asked Snow White.

"I must go to the wood and protect my treasure from the wicked dwarfs. In winter, when the earth is frozen hard, they are obliged to remain underground, for they can't work their way through; but now, when the sun has thawed and warmed the ground, they break through and come up above to spy the land and steal what they can. What once falls into their hands and into their caves is not easily brought back to light."

Snow White was quite sad over their friend's departure, and when she unbarred the door for him, the bear, stepping out, caught a piece of his fur in the door knocker, and Show White thought she caught sight of glittering gold beneath it, but she couldn't be certain of it; and the bear ran hastily away, and soon disappeared behind the trees.

A short time after this the mother sent the children into the wood to collect kindling wood. They came in their wanderings upon a big tree which lay felled on the ground, and on the trunk among the long grass they noticed something jumping up and down, but what it was they couldn't distinguish. When they approached nearer, they perceived a dwarf with a wizened face and a beard a yard long. The end of the beard was jammed into a cleft of the tree, and the little man sprang about like a dog on a chain, and didn't seem to know what he was to do. He glared at the girls with his fiery red eyes, and screamed out:

"What are you standing there for? Can't you come and help me?"

"What were you doing, little man?" asked Rose Red.

"You stupid, inquisitive goose!" replied the dwarf. "I wanted to split the tree, in order to get little chips of wood for our kitchen fire. Those thick logs that serve to make fires for coarse, greedy people like yourselves quite burn up all the little food we need. I had successfully driven in the wedge, and all was going well, but the cursed wood was so slippery that it suddenly sprang out, and the tree closed up so rapidly that I had no time to take my beautiful white beard out. So here I am stuck fast, and I can't get away; and you silly, smooth-faced, milk-and-water girls just stand and laugh! Ugh! what wretches you are!"

The children did all in their power, but they couldn't get the beard out; it was wedged in far too firmly.

"I will run and fetch somebody," said Rose Red.

"Crazy blockheads!" snapped the dwarf, "what's the good of calling anyone else? You're already two too many for me. Does nothing better occur to you than that?"

"Don't be so impatient," said Snow White, "I'll see you get help." And taking her scissors out of her pocket she cut the end off his beard.

As soon as the dwarf felt himself free he seized a bag full of gold which was hidden among the roots of the tree, lifted it up, and muttered aloud:

"Curse these rude wretches, cutting off a piece of my splendid beard!" With these words he swung the bag over his back, and disappeared without as much as looking at the children again.

Shortly after this Snow White and Rose Red went out to get a dish of fish. As they approached the stream they saw something which looked like an enormous grasshopper, springing towards the water as if it were going to jump in. They ran forward and recognized their old friend the dwarf.

"Where are you going to?" asked Rose Red. "You're surely not going to jump into the water?"

"I'm not such a fool," screamed the dwarf. "Don't you see that cursed fish is trying to drag me in?"

The little man had been sitting on the bank fishing, when unfortunately the wind had entangled his beard in the line; and when immediately afterwards a big fish bit, the feeble little creature had no strength to pull it out; the fish had the upper fin, and dragged the dwarf towards him. He clung on with all his might to every rush and blade of grass, but it didn't help him much; he had to follow every movement of the fish, and was in great danger of being drawn into the water. The girls came up just at the right moment, held him firm, and did all they could to disentangle his beard from the line; but in vain, beard and line were in a hopeless muddle. Nothing remained but to produce the scissors and cut the beard, by which a small part of it was sacrificed.

When the dwarf perceived what they were about he yelled to them:

"Do you call that manners, you toadstools! To disfigure a fellow's face? It wasn't enough that you shortened my beard before, but you must now cut off the best bit of it. I can't appear like this before my own people. I wish you'd been at Jericho first."

Then he fetched a sack of pearls that lay among the rushes, and without saying another word he dragged it away and disappeared behind a stone.

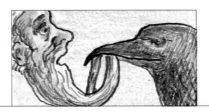

It happened that soon after this the mother sent the two girls to the town to buy needles, thread, laces, and ribbons. Their road led over a heath where huge boulders of rock lay scattered here and there. While trudging along they saw a big bird hovering in the air, circling slowly above them, but always descending lower, till at last it settled on a rock not far from them. Immediately afterwards, they heard a sharp, piercing cry. They ran forward, and saw with horror that the eagle had pounced on their old friend the dwarf, and was about to carry him off. The tender-hearted children seized ahold of the little man, and struggled so long with the bird that at last he let go of his prey. When the dwarf had recovered from the first shock he screamed in his screeching voice:

"Couldn't you have treated me more carefully? You have torn my thin little coat all to shreds, useless, awkward hussies that you are!"

Then he took a bag of precious stones and vanished under the rocks into his cave.

The girls were accustomed to his ingratitude, and went on their way and did their business in town. On their way home, as they were again passing the heath, they surprised the dwarf pouring out his precious stones on an open space, for he had thought no one would pass by at so late an hour. The evening sun shone on the glittering stones, and they glanced and gleamed so beautifully that the children stood still and gazed at them.